John H. Tatem

The Monitor of the Eastern Star

John H. Tatem

The Monitor of the Eastern Star

ISBN/EAN: 9783337411671

Printed in Europe, USA, Canada, Australia; Japan

Cover: Foto ©Andreas Hilbeck / pixelio.de

More available books at **www.hansebooks.com**

THE MONITOR

OF

THE EASTERN STAR.

CONTAINING THE

RITUAL OF ADOPTIVE MASONRY,

EMBRACED IN THE

EASTERN STAR DEGREE,

CONSISTING OF THE INITIATION, DEGREE WORK, CEREMONY
FOR OPENING AND CLOSING A LODGE, INSTALLATION
SERVICE, ETC.

Together with Forms, and Rules for the government
of Lodges.

———

Compiled and Arranged
BY *JOHN H. TATEM,*
Adrian, Mich.

———

HOLMES, COOK & BONNER, PRINTERS.
ADRIAN, MICH.

PREFACE.

The object of the compiler in the compilation of this work, is to furnish the Fraternity and friends of Adoptive Masonry, a ritual, by means of which they may be enabled to establish Lodges, and confer the Eastern Star Degree. The necessity of such a work has been suggested by the frequent requests made for a method by which Adoptive Masonry may be brought into practical use. A great amount of time and attention has been devoted by different persons in teaching Adoptive Masonry, and conferring among others the Eastern Star degree; the result of which has been to create a very warm feeling in favor of this degree, and a desire in each and every locality where it has been taught, for the establishment of a Lodge, and at the same time leaving them entirely without the means of establishing or working lodges. No work of this kind ever having been published, except the lectures appertaining to this degree, it has been found to be no easy task to arrange the work in such a manner that it could be published with some degree of secrecy, and at the same time be understood by those having a knowledge of the degree. The compiler is aware, therefore, that this work is imperfect in many respects; yet feeling desirous that the work in the various Lodges when established should be uniform, the compiler offers this volume to the friends of Adoptive Masonry, hoping that his well meant endeavors will meet with their approval.   THE COMPILER.

The objects contemplated in the establishment of the American adoptive rite, are to *associate in one common bond the worthy wives, widows, daughters and sisters of freemasons*, so as to make their adoptive privileges available for all the purposes contemplated in Masonry; to secure to them the advantages of their claim in a moral, social and charitable point of view; and from them the performance of corresponding duties.

So far as the American Adoptive rite may succeed in these, there will be cause for congratulation, whatever amount of opposition it may encounter. The communication of such degrees as "The Mason's Daughter," "The Good Samaritan," "The Heroine of Jericho,"

&c. &c , though they may answer the
temporary purposes of pleasure and
amusement, does not in any important
degree enlighten their recipients in the
inherent claim possessed by the female
relatives of Masons. Much less does it
put them in Masonic connection with
the vast brotherhood and sisterhood of
the York Rite. Least of all does it influence them in the performance of re-
ciprocal duties, without which the
Adoptive claim is an imposition.

For a wider diffusion of the Masonic
scheme of teaching morality and religion by significant *emblems;* for inclining
the influence of females towards the
York rite; for increasing social enjoy-
ment by the Masonic tie ; for ameliora-
ting the condition of widows and or-
phans; and for affording increased facil-
ities in relieving distressed travelers,
the American Adoptive rite has been
framed.

To secure successful results it is neces-

sary that its votaries should apply its
rules in a rigid sense; maintain its
Lodges valiantly; affiliate into its bonds
only those calculated by temperament
and principle, to understand and appre-
ciate it, and work out patiently and un-
tiringly its grand designs.

MEANS OF COMMUNICATION.

The means of communication and re-
cognition teach the peculiar lessons of
the rite, and enable its members to recognize each other under every circum-
stance in which they may be placed.
They are so contrived as to be easy of
acquirement and use, and consist of
signs, passes, emblems, and technical
lectures of the "Eastern Star," Degree, founded upon its traditions.
These are exceedingly beautiful and instructive. The benefits of this rite are
mainly to the female sex. For them this

temple has been reared, and these walls set up. They are its glory and crown; and its value consists in the spirit with which they enter it, and the grace they throw around it.

THE MEMBERSHIP.

The title of female members of this rite is Stellœ; that of male members, Protectors.

The lawful recipients of the American Adoptive rite are such worthy females, being wives, widows, daughters or sisters of worthy affiliated Master Masons, as may be recommended by two or more members and unanimously elected by the Lodge at its regular meeting. If unmarried they must have attained the age of eighteen years to be eligible.

Likewise, such worthy Master Masons affiliated in regular Lodges, as may be recommended by two or more members and unanimously elected as above.

The form of petition for initiation is as follows:

To the Worthy President, Vice President and Patrons of the............ Eastern Star Lodge.

The subscriber, residing in. .... aged ....years, respectfully represents that this is the....time, that.... has made application to a Lodge of the Eastern Star, and that unbiased by friends, and uninfluenced by mercenary motives,....freely and voluntarily offers ....as a candidate for initiation into the mysteries of this degree, and that ....is prompted to solicit this privilege by a favorable opinion of your ancient and honorable order, a desire of knowl edge, and a sincere wish of being serviceable to....fellow creatures. Should ....petition be granted... will cheerfully conform to all the laws, rules and regulations of the order.

Dated............A. L. 58

Recommended by

，，，，．．．．．．．．．．．．．．．．．．

．．．．．．．．．、．．．．．．．．．．．．．．

(Signed,).................

A sister or brother demitted from another Lodge and wishing to affiliate again will use the following form of petition:

To the Worthy President, Vice President and Patrons of....Lodge....of the American Adoptive Rite.

The undersigned, late member of.... Lodge, No. .... as certified by the accompanying signet of withdrawal, solicits affiliation in your Lodge.

If this petition is granted, she (he) pledges her (his) honor as a woman, (honor as a Mason) to conform, in all respects to the legal requirements of your Lodge.

Signed.................

Recommended by

....

....

The petition must be accompanied by the signet of withdrawal from the last Lodge in which the petitioner was affiliated.

Members in good standing, dssiring to change their residence, affiliate with another Lodge, or withdraw from the order, will be entitled, upon the majority vote of the members of the Lodge, to a demit in the following form:

To the Enlightened Stellœ and Protectors of the American Adoptive rite, this Demit witnesseth:

That sister (Bro.) A. B., was initiated into the light of Adoptive Masonry, (or affiliated into the membership) of the Eastern Star in this Lodge, on the.... day of....18....

That during her (his) connection with us, she (he) has, in all respects, conformed to the legal requirements of this Lodge. That in her withdrawal she (he) bears with her (him) the love and esteem of the officers and members of this Lodge and we do hereby most affectionately commend her (him) to the kindly offices and friendship of all enlightened Stellæ and Protectors wherever in the journey of human life she (he) may be found.

(Signed.)   W. P.......... ...

                    Vice P... . ...

(Seal.)   Sec........ .. ....

THE BUSINESS OF THE LODGE.

The business of the Lodge is to act upon petitions; to initiate; to dispense charity and sympathy; to confer the degree of the Eastern Star and communicate the lectures of the same; to exercise discipline; likewise to take all proper measures for cultivating peace and harmony, and extending the Christian principles of morality and love among the members. Finally, to aid in the important work of extending the benefits of the American Adoptive rite to every community where there are persons entitled to receive it.

The meetings of a Lodge are stated and called. The stated meetings are those enjoined by the by-laws, and may be held either weekly, semi-monthly, monthly or quarterly at the choice of the members, expressed in the by-laws.

The called meetings are those summoned at the will of the W. P. or in the absence of that officer, by the V. P., upon any emergency apparent to him.

The paraphernalia essential to the meetings of the Lodge, are one or more bibles, membership board and by-laws. To these should be added, when convenient. the banner of the Lodge, a key, and other appliances for work and instruction.

Those precautionary measures which form so prominent a feature in all secret affiliated systems, whereby they are enabled to detect imposters and reject them from their assemblies, are of the highest possible importance in the American Adoptive Rite, in view of the peculiar intimacy between the sexes, which constitutes the prime feature and aim of this society. This intimacy is, in itself, well calculated to furnish the world with a subject for slanderous imputations; and it will infallibly render any negligence allowed, though apparently slight and unimportant, serious in its consequences.

The officers of the Lodge are therefore enjoined by every principle of prudence and self-preservation, to study critically the standard measures of precaution; to exercise extraordinary vigilance in purging their assemblies; and to allow neither fear nor favor to bias them in the admission of unworthy or unenlightened visitors.

OPENING THE LODGE.

The hour for opening the Lodge having arrived, the W. P. repairs to the East, calls the Lodge to order, and requests the officers to repair to their stations and proceed as follows:

Brother Sentinel you will approach the East. Your duties will require you to remain without, guarding with all diligence the entrance to this place, and suffering neither fear nor favor to influence you, in admitting improper visitors. Will you perform this trust in truth and vigilance?

Sentinel—What guarantee have I that in my absence the work of the Lodge will be performed agreeably to the usages of the American Adoptive Rite?

W. P.—The honor of an Adoptive Mason.

Sentinel—It is well. I accept it, and if you will furnish me with the means of security, I will guard you with truth and vigilance while here assembled.

W. P.—Receive the implement of your office and repair to your station.

W. P.—S g w a t f d o y o. Guard —T s t t a o a a d g. W. President— Y w s t w a d g a i t s t w a a t r l i t d a d h t a n t a t i d u n o m r t r t.— Guard—W a d g w P. W. President— B v P a y s t a p a b a s o t e s d. Vice President—I a n s w p b w i b t a o s s a t p s s a t p y w p t t L a s t a p a i p o t p a e t a s i t l. I a n s w P t a p a b a s o t e s a e t s i t l. W. President— B v p a y a b o t e s. Vice President— I h s h s i t e. W. President—F w c y h. Vice President—I h c t w. W. President—H y t c w. Vice President — I h. W. President—W y g i t m. Vice

President—I w w y a, wp, b, vp, n y b, wp, b y vp f w p a vp t w p a v p l f W P. h t w a s vp i h t f i w b f t t c o a b o s f t w s r t s o t d u s e o t l s f o o m w w w f t c m. W. President—H y t c m vp i h wp w y g i m vp i w w y a wp b vp n y b wp b y vp f w p a vp t wp a v p l. W. President—W i t g p i t l. Vice President—A t r o t vp. W. President—S g w a t d o y o. Guard—T c m f o o t a a s t t a o a a d g. W. President—W i t f p p i t l. Guard—A t r a i f o t c. W. President—S f p w a t d o y o. 1st Patron—T i c i t p o t r a t J d. W. President—W i t s p p i t l. 1st Patron—A t l a i f o t vp. W. President—S s p w a t d o y o. 2d Patron—T i c i t p o t r a t r. W. President—W i t t p p i t l. 2d Patron—A t r a i t o t v p. W. President—S t p w a t d o y o. 3d Patron—T i c i t p o t r a t e. W. President—W i t f p p i t l. 3d Patron—I t s. W. President —S f p w a t d o y o. 4th Patron—T i

2

18

citpotratm. W. President—Wi
tfppitl. 4th Patron—At l a i f o t
wp. W. President—S f p w a t d o y
o. 5th Patron—T i c i t p o t r a t e.
W. President—W i t s p i t l. 5th Patron—A t l o t w p. W. President—s s
W a t d o y o Sec t k a r o t p o t l r a
m d t l p t o t t t h r t. W. President
—W i t t p i t l Sec a t r o t e. W.
President—S t w a t d o y o. Treasurer—T r a m d t l f t h o t s k a j a o
t s p t o b o o t W. P. w t c o t l. W.
President—W i t c p i t l. Treasurer—
A t r o t w P. W. President—S c w a
t d o y o. C t r c a c t t t v r o t r t i a a v.
W. President—W i t v p p i t l. Conductor—I t w. W. President—B v p
w a t d o y o. Vice President—
T a t W P i t g o t l a t a t o t c. W.
President—T p p i t l. Vice President—I t e W P. W. President.—W
a t d o h o. Vice President—T p o t
d o t l a g t s a o c d p o o a c s f i t
c a t h m s p. W. President—(C u t l

a s) B & S t w t s (p b t c.) W. President—B a s o t e s i i m o t t l n r l a b
d o f s b a m r c b i y w p t n o t o a c y
a b m o t m f s g y w i t s.

At closing the Lodge a similar ceremony takes place; the avenues of the
Lodge are again carefully guarded; a
re-capitulation of the duties of the officers is rehearsed. It is particularly essential that each member should become
familiar with the ceremony of opening
and closing the Lodge in due form.
Especially should those who have the
honor to preside over the Lodge, be
well qualified to discharge the duties in-
cumbent on their positions A suitable
hymn concludes the ceremony, after
which the W. President declares the
Lodge closed in due form.

CLOSING HYMN.

Music—"SWEET HOME."

Farewell till again we shall welcome the time,
· Which brings us once more to our fame cherished
  shrine ;
And though from each other we distant may roam,
  Again may all meet in this, our dear-loved home.

  Home, home—Sweet, sweet home ;
  May sisters and brothers find joy and peace at
  home.

And when our last parting on earth shall draw nigh,
  And we shall be called to the Grand Lodge on high ;
May each be prepared when the summons shall come,
To meet the Grand Master in Heaven, our home.

  Home, home—sweet, sweet home,
  May sisters and brothers find joy and peace at
  home.

After the Lodge is opened in due form at a regular communication, the following order of business will be observed :

1st. Calling roll of Officers.

2d. Reading minutes of preceeding meeting.

3d. Reading and referring petitions.

4th. Reports of Committees on Applications.

5th. Balloting on Applications.

6th. Conferring Degrees.

7th. Reports of Special Committees.

8th. Receiving and considering resolutions.

9th. Considering unfinished business.

10th. New Business.

11th. Closing the Lodge.

THE INITIATION—INTRODUCTORY RE-MARKS.

The ceremonial of initiations into the American Adoptive Rite is not reckoned a Degree, but rather a mental preparation and trial of the temper and spirit of the applicants, preparatory to their being favored with the full light of the adoption. One weeks time must be given between the initiation and the degree, save where by a vote of the lodge permission for a more rapid advancement is given.

The system of initiations comprises the whole of the covenant of adoption, which must be carefully explained to the applicants before requring them to receive it. It is requisite, in general, if the candidate is a lady, that she have one or two of her female friends with her, members of the order, to bear her company in the ante-room, until she enters the Lodge. But the presence of her husband, father or brother may be substituted in case the membership of the Lodge is too small to spare the ladies from the room.

In considering a petition for the light of Adoptive Masonry, let these four points of inquiry be made:

1st. Is the petition in due form; signed by the applicants own hand, re commended by the constitutional number, and accompanied by the fee required by the By-Laws.

2d. Is the applicant a suitable subject for the American Adoptive Rite; if a lady, eighteen years of age and upwards the wife, widow, daughter or sister of an affiliated master mason in good standing; if a gentleman, an affiliated master mason in good standing.

3d. Is the applicant perfectly acceptable to every officer and member of the Lodge, so far as can be known.

4th. Is the applicant of sound mind and capable of acquiring a knowledge of this Rite.

The petition having been thus thoroughly considered, the vote must be taken by secret ballot and the result recorded by the Secretary. If the ballot is favorable, the petitioner may at once be initiated. If not an interval of at least three months must elapse before the application can be renewed.

INITIATORY SERVICE.

The applicant, if a lady, being elected and in waiting, a communication to that effect is made by the Sentinel, the vice President then retires to the ante-room with the petition in his hand, introduces himself to the candidate as an official member of the Lodge, and thus addresses her :

V. P.—Are you the lady whose name is appended to this petition.

Applicant—I am.

V. P.—Do you still entertain the desire expressed in this petition to receive the light of Adoptive Masonry.

Applicant—I do.

V. P.—Who will be responsible to the Lodge for the good faith of this lady.

Sentinel—By my knowledge of the Masonic brethren who have recommended her petition, I will.

V. P.—It is well; I accept it.

It behooves me then as one of the officers of this Lodge, to instruct you in the general nature of the covenant of adoption and explain to you the first and second portions of it,—t c i t s p o p w y m m b y c b a i o o,—B w d n w y t m i, n w w p y t m i, s w y o c a w a f u o w i i b i,—L t m t a a I a d s y b u t b y t s y m w i o o r f t p. The objects for which we are banded together are to comfort, protect and aid each other through the labyrinth of human life, and make its hardships light by means of cheerful companionship and social pleasures. We are willing you should join us in this pleasing work.

We are in possession of certain signs, passes, ceremonies, and lectures, by means of which we recognize each other wherever we go. We are willing to make you acquainted with these secrets that you, too, may be recognized as an Adoptive Mason.

We are governed by certain rules, regulations and by-laws, framed by ourselves. We are bound by these rules, regulations, and by-laws, so long as we remain members of the Soci·ety. I t o w s e y t s.—W a t t a s a m o t o: a b w c a f a d o o t a m o r. —y w i l m b p u r.

We are all of us, in faith Christians, and it is a large part of the business of this Society to rehearse the life and doc-trines of Christ, and endeavor to imitate and practice upon his example. I this faith and in these works you, too, will be expected to participate.

I t a t t f e t y t y w n b w t p A, t i n, V P, d y t, c y h a a w a y t a a b i t b, t y w n r o s a t y w b o t t r r, a b l o o s, A I d.

V. P.—It is well, give us admittance to the Lodge.

Conductor—W m d f t o L, T r y b u h c u t y a a p s f t l o a m w t t l w s t y h w b p a i y. Human life is a labyrinth through which we wander too often, alas, blindly and in ignorance. It is good for us to have a friendly hand that can guide us with infallible certainty and safety through its most intricate mazes. Such a companion may be found in Jesus Christ; who lived as we are living, died as we must die, and went before us to Heaven to prepare a place for us. P m h o t p o t a a y g t a l w o y c n p a t l y t t p o o e c o.—B r f o a t c o t d g o l (C h h a s b w s

g w b h a c i f o t b.) T l i t p. (A t
p t s o t v P t a a.)

V. P. W b t—C—I k n—V P y k n
—C b i h a h—V P—w h t t—C Charity
V. P.—It is well. I b m n a o o t o o
t l t i y i t t s o t c o a. The society of
Adoptive Masonry is bound together by
ties of mutual aid and relief. We coun-
sel each other when in difficulty; sympathise with each other when in afflic-
tion; and give aid to each other when
in distress. A y w t c y h a a w a y t
a a b i t b t y w n r o s a t y w
b o t t r r a b o o s. A. I a V.
P.—It is well; Adoptive Masons de-
rive their knowledge from the pages of
the b v y b, have learned that we are
exposed through every moment of our
lives, to be led away by temptations.
We pray that we may not be led into
temptation. We encourage each other
to resist temptation. A w a s p n t d
a i t o a b w o a. A w a s i d h u w t s
w w r t m o j d o R E m a e a o y m s

t r. b r o o c o a a r w t p t t s r h p r.
B s i b s (e s) a y w t c y h a a w a y t
a a b i t b t y w t a z p w u i t w. A i a.
V. P.—t i w p C. A t p t s o t C t h.
C t i t s w i h v f a t t i m a y w s t o L.
We are taught in the lessons of Adoptive Masonry to resign, at times, our
comforts and ease, that by so doing we
can benefit our fellow creatures. B. S.
(t c t t v c) s m y b e m d f t f t o s o s
i o o. Whenever wearied on the journey of human life, may you always find
as now you do, a friend who has a place,
and a heart to refresh you, r n a l u b g,
—a t p t s o t f p t a a—f p, w b t, C i k n F
P y k n—C b i h a h—F P. w h t t, C a.
F P. i i w p a—S P, w b t. C i k n. S p
y k n C, b i h a h, S P, w h t t C a S P,
i i w p a T P. w b t. C i k n T P, y k n.
C, b i h a h T P, w h t t. C. C, T P, i i
w p C—F P, w b t. C i k n F P. y k n. C
b i h a h F P, w h t t. C. D. F P, i i w i b m
n, a o o t o o t l t i y i t f s o t c o a.
The society of Adoptive Masonry is a

society of Christians. None enter our ranks save those who believe that Jesus Christ is the Son of God, the Redeemer of the World, and the Almighty Savior. We teach no lessons but such as relate to him. We make no prayers but through His holy name. We entertain no religious hopes but those which are founded upon his Birth, Life, Death, Resurrection and Ascension. A y w t c y h a a w a y t a a b i t b t y w t a z p w u i t w o p t t. A, i a—F P, i i w p D—F P, w b t. C, i k n—F P, y k n. C, b i h a h—F P, w h t t. C. F.—F P, i i w p f, (a t p t s o t B t h.) C t i t s p o y r B. S. C, You are now very near the end of our labyrinth, and so are you not far from the end of human life. Above you is suspended the banner of our order, the Lion of the Tribe of Judah. Under the shadow of this Rock may you dwell. And when in the last stages of the labyrinth of life, old age shall admonish you of your speedy end, may you be revived by the unfailing strength of Him whom you have faithfully served, r, l u b g (t p i f o t W. P.) W. P. w b t. C. Hopes, Hopes, many and bright, a field of virtues in which the principles of our order may produce an abundant harvest. W. P. It is well; may they be amply realized. A t t m i b m a t c o o t l t b y m s (b) t u a t o o b t c o a, t c w e t y, m s a v s o y j, y c t r i, y, e n i y h a r t m t s p, w w r y f y p, a p y t w. I w r i t y, l y m i a m b d. 1st; y a c t p i s a i s a t c l s a p b t t a a r. 2d; y a c t o t c a a t r r a, b l o t l o w y m b a m. 3d; y a l t d t y s a b a i t t s i t s a a i t p. 4th; t y a c t a s y s o b o p a a o i o u t t. 5th; y a f t e t m y l u t c l u b o l j c. D y t a t p c y h, a a w, a y t a a b i t b. A, i d.

W. P. It is well. We readily accept the pledge you make us. We share with you in this covenant, and do now accept you into our band. Sister Secretary,

make record that Sister............ the
............of Brother... .... an
affiliated Master Mason, is now initiated
into the American Adoptive Rite. Sisters, give her a kind assurance of her
welcome among us, (t f p a a t t e b t
h w w o w a p.)

W. P. My sister, we hail with true
pleasure your coming amonst us. The
work of Adoptive Masonry is amply
sufficient for us all, and we shall rejoice
to find you excelling in your zeal that of
the most devoted members of our Society.

We are laboring to increase our own
happiness and to promote that of others.
Our experience and the wisdom we
gain from the Scriptures, alike teach us
that this world is a harsh, unfriendly
scene, poorly adapted to impart felicity,
and that it is chiefly by combining the
efforts of the good and true, in the work
of morality and religion, that happiness is
to be acquired and extended. The

greater our ability to do good, the more pleasure we shall enjoy.

We meet in private, that we may arrange our plans for the good work in which we are engaged, without interruption from those who cannot understand or sympathise with us. In our meetings we strive to learn our duty as beings who possess an immortal part, and when we return home it is our care to perform it. We cultivate a spirit of harmony, that the enemy of souls may acquire no advantage over us.

And as a large portion of our work as Adoptive Masons lies in acquiring the doctrines and temper of Jesus Christ, whom truly to know is everlasting life. We often unite to address the Heavenly Throne and to plead with God that the very spirit of faith and wisdom may descend upon us, and make our our meeting place a place like Heaven. In such a prayer let us now with cheerful faith combine.

Source of all Wisdom, Truth and Love, grant to us that, in the reception of these persons, we may add strength to our strength, and grace to our grace. Oh! may the golden chain thus lengthened become the brighter for these links, and be strengthened for the great work we do. Enlarge our powers to benefit mankind and to honor God, and when, one by one, each link shall fall away in death, may the parting be temporary and the meeting eternal. In the world where death comes not, may we realize the full happiness of loving and serving Thee forever. We ask through Christ the Saviour, Amen.

EASTERN STAR DEGREE.

The Lodge having been opened in due form, and the candidate in waiting in the ante-room, the alarm is given in the usual way, when the Guard responds.as follows:

A candidate desiring to be initiated into the mysteries of the Eastern Star Degree.

W. P. Sister Conductor, you will repair to the ante-room, receive the candidate, and conduct her through the various requisitions of the Ritual.

(A t c e t r a b t c t L i c u w a n i s s a s f t o a t c i b c t t a t r h i f o t v P.)

Vice P. W c h C a c d t b i i t m o t c s d. Vice P. Sister A. B. We take it as a compliment to Freemasons that you have expressed a desire to unite yourself with our order. The benefits of this Degree are mainly to the female sex. and I am free to inform you that you are at this time connected to Masonry by ties far more intimate and tender than you are aware of, or than I can even inform you of. The widow and orphan daughter of a Master Mason, takes the place of the husband and father, in the affections and good deeds of the Lodge. If their character is unjustly assailed (and oh! how often the character of the most virtuous and pure, is assailed by the foul tongue of slander ?) the brethren will defend them. If they are in want, distressed for the necessities of life, the brethren will divide their means with them. If traveling at a distance from home, they find themselves sick and in want, among strangers, they have but to make themselves known as the widow or the orphan daughter of a Worthy Master Mason, and lo! the hand of relief is stretched out toward them. The voice of sympathy is heard to cheer them; they are no longer strangers, but friends, dear friends, and thus they are constrained to bless our Society, whose kind deeds are not confined to the narrow limits of home.

This is no fancy sketch. It is what has happened—what is happening every day. The widow has been provided with a home; her children educated and reared up to honorable stations in society, her own heart cheered and comforted by the blessed influences of Masonry; and this so often in every Lodge in the land, that were it our custom to publish abroad such things, a volume might be made up every year of these deeds of heavenly beneficence.

These are but a few of the reasons why we think the Ladies should be the most devoted friends that Masonry possesses. To them is given all the advantages of the Society, its shield of protection, its hand of relief, and its voice of sympathy, while we do not require of them any of the labor or expense of sustaining it. A y t w t o y s t c t a t l r a r g t l a a b a s o t e s d. A, i a V P D y s d u y h a a w (o a a m m) t y w n r t s o t d u, –T y w n b p n a i c t d u a m n v f a b a m m n u a w n v f a b t w w s o d o a m m — F t y w r t n o a w b o s o t d t a t y a s a y d t w a f a t n m r a y a p—F t y w n s d o a w b o s o t d b t b b w g t d a t n t t m w o a d.—A, i a V P y h m p t p o.

The candidate is then conducted to the station of the First Patron.

1st P.—w c h—C. a c d t b i i t p o t r a t j d.

1st Patron. Jephthah was Governor of Israel and Commander of the armies of the Lord. He was a pious man, and as our traditions say, a Freemason. Going out on one occasion, at the head of his armies, he prayed most earnestly to God for victory, and made a vow—a rash and unfortunate vow, as it afterwards proved—that if his prayer was answered, and he should return home in triumph, he would offer as a sacrifice whatever should meet him coming out of his dwelling. His prayer was heard, a splendid victory was given him, and he returned home at the head of his army rejoicing.

When he arrived at the brow of the hill above his house he paused for a moment, for now he anxiously recalled to mind his vow, and he waited to see what should first come from his doors. He expected it would be his daughter's pet lamb. But imagine his distress, conceive his anguish and horror when he beheld his daughter, his only child, a fair young maiden, just emerging into womanhood, come forth, and in the joy of meeting her father, run to meet him with singing and dances. He fell on his face in the dust. He rent his clothes, and in the anguish of his heart cried aloud: " Alas, my daughter, thou hast brought me very low!"

When his daughter was informed of his vow, and that her life or his dishonor was its penalty, she hesitated not a moment to confirm it. She only said, " My father, if indeed thou hast opened thy mouth unto the Lord, turn not back." She made this one request, *that he would give her two months' time to prepare herself for her terrible fate.* It was granted •and she went in company with her female friends, among the caves of the mountains, where they mourned unceasingly, day and night, her impending death.

When the two months had expired, and the day arrived which was to bring this sad affair to a close, a vast multitude gathered together to witness the event. Many thought that Jephthah's daughter would refuse to come and submit to so frightful a doom. But precisely as the sun came on the meridian, she was seen followed by a long train of her friends, winding her way down the mountain side, to the fatal spot where the altar was erected, and her father, with an almost broken heart, was standing, prepared to fulfil his vow.

She approached him and with one long kiss of affection bade him farewell. Taking up the thick mourning veil which she had worn, he threw it gently over her face and drew his sword. But she rapidly unveiled herself, and said she needed not to have her face covered, for *she was not afraid to die.* Her father replied that he could not strike the blow while she looked upon him, and again cast it over her. She threw it off the second time, and turning from him, said she would look up to the heavens, so that his hand should not be unnerved by the sight of her face, but that *she would not consent to die in the dark.* A third time, however, he insisted, and a third time she as resolutely cast it off, this time holding the ends of it firmly in her hands, and then in the hearing of the multitude she solemnly declared that if this ceremony was insisted upon, she would claim the protection of the law and refuse the fate that otherwise she was willing to endure. She said it was the practice to cover the faces of murderers and criminals when they were about to be put to death, but for her part *she was no criminal, and died only to redeem her father's honor.* Again she averred that she would cast her eyes upward upon the source of Light, and in that position she invited the fatal blow. It fell. Her gentle spirit mounted to the heavens upon which her last gaze had been fixed, and so the deed was consummated which has rendered the name of Jephthah's Daughter forever famous in the annals of Scripture and of Masonry.

[*Here explain again, and carefully, the sign of Jephthah's Daughter, and the manner in which the pass is given.*]

JEPHTHAH'S DAUGHTER.---Judges xi: 35,

Air.— " Love Not."

Father! father! the joyful minstrel sung—
　Lo, glad I come, with timbrel and with dance!
Hail. father, hail! thine arm in God was strong!
　Hail, God of Israel, Israel's sure defense!
　　　　Hosanna! hosanna!
　　　　　　　Thus the minstrel sung.

Father! father! the astonished daughter said—
　What grief is this, what means this sign of woe?
Dust on thy head? thy gray hairs floating wide?
　That look of horror on each soldier's brow?
　　　　Bewailing! bewailing—
　　　　　　　Thus the daughter cried.

Father! father! the astonished daughter cried—
　If thus I'm doomed, if thus thy vow has gone,
Turn not thou back! there's hope amidst the dead,
　None to the perjured—let thy will be done!
　　　　Hosanna! hosanna!
　　　　　　　Thus the maiden said.

Father! father! the doomed one meekly spoke—
　Be strong thy hand, be resolute thy heart!
To Heaven's re-union I will joyful look,
　And with a blessing on thy head depart!
　　　　Farewell! farewell!
　　　　　　　Thus the doomed one spoke.

They now pass to the station of 2d Patron.

2d P.—W c h C a c d i i t p o t r a t r.

2d P—The Scriptural account of Ruth is one of the most beautiful, tender and touching passages in Holy Writ. It is as interesting to the young as to the old, and opens up to us the most complete account of the usages of ancient society, thirteen hundred years before the coming of Christ, that we possess. But when enlightened by the traditions of Masonry, as given in the Eastern Star Degree, it is still more interesting.

Ruth was of the nation of Moab, a people of idolators. She married a man of God, by whose pious example and teachings she was converted to the true religion. Upon his death bed he charged her, for her soul's sake to leave the dangerous company in which she would be thrown, and go to the city of Bethlehem, where dwelt the people of God. His name was Mahlon, and our traditions inform us that he was a Freemason.

Immediately after his death she obeyed his pious injunctions. Forsaking her home and friends, she journeyed in company with her aged mother in-law, to Bethlehem, and arrived in due time, but way-worn and so poor that she was compelled, for her own support and that of her friend, to seek some means of securing a livelihood. There was nothing, however, that she could do, save to go into the barley fields,—for it was the time of harvest,—and glean among the poorest and lowest classes of the people for a support. The very first attempt she made at this labor, exhausted her strenth. She had been reared in luxury and the toil was too great for her. The sharp stubble wounded her feet. The blazing sun oppressed her brain. The jeers and insults of her companions alarmed and discouraged her, and long before the hour of noon, with only two little handsful of barley, as the fruits of

her labor she sought the shade of a tree
to refresh herself for a few moments, before retiring from the field.

At this instant, Boaz, the owner of
the field, entered. He was a pious and
charitable man, and as our traditions say
a Freemason. None in Bethlehem so
rich, none more beloved and honored
than he. As he entered the field, he
observed near the gleaners the form
of one different in garb and manners
from the rest, and asked the over-
seer who she was? In reply he
learned that she was a woman from
Moab, who had asked leave to glean
among the sheaves, but that evidently
she was unaccustomed to such labor, for
she had been there since the sunrise and
had gathered but two little handsful of
barley. This excited the kindly feelings
of Boaz, and he went to her to say
words of sympathy, and to offer her relief

As she saw him approach, she sup-
posed him to be the owner of the field,

and come to order her away, as a vaga-
bond or a thief. Ever since the morning she had met with nothing but scorn
and reproach, and she looked for it now.
Raising her hands, therefore, to show
him how small were her gleanings, and
that she had stolen nothing from the
sheaves, she crossed them meekly upon
her breast, as showing her willingness
to submit to whatever lot she might be
called upon to endure, and cast her eyes
upward as appealing to God against the
inhumanity of man. It was for God she
had forsaken home, wealth and friends,
and the disconsolate widow, alone in
the wide world, had none other to whom
she could look for protection. This mute
appeal was not lost to the kind heart of
Boaz. He spoke words of sympathy
and tenderness to her. He encouraged
her to persevere. From the provisions
brought for his reapers he ordered her
to eat and drink. He directed that handsful of barley should be dropped in her

way by the reapers, that she might gather an ample supply, so that when she returned to her mother-in law, she bore with her as much as she would.

The Masonic history of Ruth ends here; but the scriptural account goes on to say that she became the wife of this generous man and Mason, and that through a long line of posterity, Christ, according to the flesh, was her son! She was the grandmother of Jesse, the father of David, the father of Solomon, whose wisdom and might are known equally to every Bible reader and to every intelligent Mason.

From Moab's hills the stranger comes,
　By sorrow tried, widowed by death—
She comes to Judah's goodly homes,
　Led by the trusting hand of faith.
　　　Ye friends of God a welcome lend
　　　　The fair and virtuous Ruth to day:
　　　A generous heart and hand extend,
　　　　And wipe the widow's tears away.

She leaves her childhood's home, and all
　That brothers, friends and parents gave;
The flowery fields, the lordly hall,
　The green sod o'er her husband's grave.
　　　Ye friends of God, &c., &c.

She leaves the gods her people own;
  Soulless and weak, they're hers no more;
JEHOVAH, He is God alone,
  And Him her spirit will adore.
    Ye friends of God, &c., &c.

At Bethlehem's gates the stranger stands,
  All friendless, poor and wanting rest;
She seeks the aid of loving hands
  And liberal hearts that God has blest.
    Ye friends of God, &c., &c.

They now pass to the station of the 3d Patron.

Third Patron—w c h—C–a c d i i t p o t r a t e.—

3d P.—The history of Esther is that of a heroine, inspired by the noblest sentiments of religion, to offer her life to save the people of God from destruction, or in the event of failure, to perish with them. The scriptural account of Esther, found in the Book of Esther, is beautiful and instructive; but still more so when enlightened by the traditions of Masonry.

Esther was reared up in obscurity, among the exiled people of Israel, then

4

dwelling in the land of Persia. Her beauty and virtue, and still more, her intellectual endowments attracted the attention of the king, the mighty Ahasuerus, who made her his wife and queen, presented her with a splendid palace, and honored her above all the women of the land.

The more intimately he became acquainted with her mental powers, the more he admired them. There was no question so difficult she could not aid him to solve; no subject so intricate she could not assist him to unravel. In time he made her his confidant in all the affairs of the kingdom; and in the consideration of every question, she proved herself a true descendant of the wise king Solomon. All the traditions of that period prove that Esther was one of the most remarkable women who ever graced the pages of history.

The traditions of Freemasonry inform us that the king Ahasuerus was a Freemason. He was a man who chiefly valued himself upon keeping his word. The almighty power and importance of truth was to him an object of frequent contemplation. You will not be surprised therefore, when you hear the sequel of this singular history.

The enemies of the Jews, who were very numerous and powerful, had brought the most bitter and false accusations before the king, and had induced him to pass an edict that on a certain day the entire nation should be exterminated. Every man, woman and child of these unfortunate exiles was to be put to death, and thus the chosen people of God totally blotted out from the earth. But God appointed queen Esther an instrument to prevent so great a calamity.

No sooner did she learn of this cruel edict, than she resolved to use her influence with the king to save her nation, and if she failed, to perish with them. The king had often promised her that whenever she came before him robed and adorned as a queen, and made any request of him whatever, he would grant it, " even to the half of the kingdom." Now was the time to test his sincerity. So devoted to truth as he was, she could not hesitate to make her appeal to him now. She devoted herself to prayer and fasting for three days and nights, and then causing herself to be attired in the silken robes, and with the crown of her royal state, she went boldly through the streets of the city to the palace of the king.

It was a day of state. The king was engaged in giving public reception to the governors of the many nations under his rule, and his audience-chamber was crowded with the dignitaries of the kingdom. Esther was stopped by the sentinels at the gate, and informed that by a law of the palace, no person, under penalty of death, could enter the king's presence unless first summoned. Of this, however, she was aware, and passed on, as it were, with her life in her hands.

The scene, as this heroic woman entered the audience-chamber, was magnificent. All that could render such an occasion brilliant, was there, from the king on his throne, radiant with jewels, to the gorgeous equipage of the officers and decorations of the apartment. In contrast with all their splendid array, stood Queen Esther, pale with long fasting and emotion, who strove to catch the eye of the king. As she did so, he rose, confused and angry that the law of the palace had been violated. At that instant Esther placed her hand upon the crown she wore, and upon the robe, and thus tacitly reminded him of his solemn promise. He remembered his pledge, and calling her to him at the foot of the throne, held out his golden scepter, that by placing her hand upon it, an evident sign of pardon and acceptance might be seen by all present. Then he said

"WHAT WILT THOU, Queen Esther? And what is thy request? It shall be given thee, even to the half of the kingdom."

The Masonic history of Esther ends here, but the scriptural account goes on to say that at a proper time she made known her request, which was granted by the king, and the whole nation of the Jews was thereby saved. Not one life was sacrificed, and to this day the Jewish people keep one day in each year as a festival to commemorate the boldness, intelligence and fidelity of Queen Esther.

(*Here explain again, and carefully, the sign of Esther, and the manner in which the pass is given.*)

ESTHER.--Esther v : 3.

Queen of Persia's broad domain,
  Why this anguish and despair?
Blinding tears like falling rain;
  Sighs and words of hopeless prayer!

Round thee stands a waiting train,
  Wealth and beauty, rank and power—
All to bring relief is vain,
  Queen of sadness, in this hour.

For a voice has gone abroad,
  Stern and fearful, filied with doom,
Israel's exiles to the sword,
  Sword and brand to Israel's home.

Lo, that high, expressive brow—
  Grand—but what woman do;
Hark. those words the purpose show—
  " I will save or perish too! "

" To the Sovereign I will haste—
  Robe your queen in purity—
Crown her as in triumphs past—
  Maidens, to the throne with me."

Queen, thy holy aim is won;
  God o'errules the stern decree—
Sends a pardon from the throne,
  Israel saves, and honors thee.

They now pass to the station of the Fourth Patron. 4th P.—w c h C a c d i i t p o t r a t m.

4th P.—The history of Martha is that of a young woman oppressed with grief at the loss of an only brother, yet keeping, amidst death and every discouragement, an unshaken faith in the promises of Christ. Martha and Mary were sisters who dwelt with their brother, Lazarus. The traditions of our Society inform us that he was a Freemason. The three lived together in great harmony, and were favored above all the citizens of Bethany, by being the friends of Jesus Christ, who, in his frequent visits to that village, made their dwelling his abiding place. They were known by their neighbors as the disciples of him to whom they showed so many marks of affection.

On one occasion, when Christ was absent from Bethany, Lazarus was taken suddenly and violently sick. The case admitted of no delay, and the afflicted sisters dispatched a messenger to the place where Christ was, with their wishes expressed in these words, "Lord, behold! he whom thou lovest is sick!"— They might well have thought that such an appeal would have brought their Divine friend to their aid in the greatest haste, and that the life of Lazarus might thus be saved. But though the messenger returned, Jesus did not come. Lazarus grew worse, while the sisters listened for the feet of their expected guest, —and died. He was taken immediately to the sepulchre according to the custom of the country, and these mourning females felt that they were alone. Their brother dead! Their friend, upon whose miraculous power they had relied so greatly, a deserter in their greatest time of need! What had they to live for now!

But Christ, though apparently negligent to their call, knew better than they what was best for them. He was but trying their faith, and that dead man, sleeping in his gloomy sepulchre, was but a part of the trial. At the end of the fourth day, Martha, who had never ceased to look towards Jerusalem, with a half hope that he would yet come and bring peace to their wounded hearts, heard the message, "the Master is coming," and ran eagerly to the edge of the village to greet him. She fell on her knees before him, and with her hands upraised in an attitude of supplication, and in soft and loving words, rebuked the tardiness which had cost her brother's life. Looking into his face, she saw the gentle smile there, which always spoke of hope and mercy, and was soon constrained to add, 'But I know that even now, whatsoever thou wilt ask of God, God will give it thee."

Jesus saith unto her, "Thy brother shall rise again."

Martha replied, " I know that he shall

rise again in the resurrection at the last day."

Jesus saith unto her, " I am the resurrection and the life; he that believeth in me, though he were dead, yet shall he live; and whosoever liveth and believeth in me shall never die. BELIEVEST THOU THIS?

Thus the Saviour tried the faith of Martha. Did she believe that he had the power, then and there, to raise her brother from the dead? That was the meaning of his question. It would have been a hard one to others, but not to her. She answered at once, in the tone and spirit of perfect faith, " Yea Lord, I believe that thou art the Christ, the son of God, which should come unto the world!"

The reward of such faith was soon rendered. Taking her by the hand, and passing by their dwelling where they were joined by Mary, they went to the sepulchre, and as every scripture reader knows, Jesus raised the dead man to life.

(Here explain again, and carefully, the sign of Martha, and the manner in which the pass is given.)

MARTHA.---John xi : 26.

Air.—"THE SOLDIER'S TEAR.

Low in the dust she knelt,
  Down by the Saviour's feet,
With weeping eyes and hands upraised,
  Up to the mercy seat ;
The friendless girl was sad—'
  Complainingly she sighed—
Oh, hadst thou come while yet he lived,
  Our brother had not died.

The Saviour's gentle smile,
  New hopes in Martha woke:
Thy brother he shall rise again,
  The gracious Saviour spoke.
The living shall not die,
  If in me they believe,
And though they in the dust may lie,
  The very DEAD shall live.

Into the Master's face,
  The sad one meekly gazed:

There is no fear in love, there is
  No doubt where faith is placed.
Thou art, thou art, the Christ—
  In thee the dead shall live—
Whatever thou shalt ask of God,
  I know that God will give.

Before an open tomb,
  A joyful group is seen:
The grave has yielded up its dead,
  And faith once more is green.
No longer tears are thine,
  Sweet Martha, soul of faith,
Thy love for Christ has found reward,
  Thy brother won from death.

They now pass to the station of the Fifth patron. 5th P.—w e h—C a e d i i t p o t r a t e.

5th Patron.—The last of these five female characters, whose virtues and misfortunes make up the glory of the Eastern Star, is Electa No account of this celebrated woman is given in the scriptures; we are entirely indebted for what we know of her to Masonic tradition. Her husband's name was Gaius, and he was long *Grand Master of Masons,* in which situation he was succeeded by the illustrious John the Evangelist. Electa had been reared up amongst a heathen people, and like the rest, had been taught to worship idols, in which faith she had reared her children. But happening by good chance to hear a discourse from the Christian Missionary, Paul, she, with her husband and all her family, yielded their faith to him whose gospel was so powerfully imparted to them, and they became Christians.

It was at a period when all manner of persecutions awaited those who professed the Christian faith. Imprisonment, scourgings, loss of property and often the loss of life was the price paid by those who gave in their adhesion to Christ. Electa and her family, however were spared for many years. The Masonic influence which her husband so largely shared, made friends amongst those who would otherwise have persecuted them; and although they were often scourged and pointed at as the followers of a crucified Saviour, yet no other evil befell them.

In adopting the Christian religion, Electa had adopted all the virtues and graces that flow out of it. To spend her large income in relieving the poor; to devote much of her time to the care of the sick; to keep an open house for indigent and hungry travelers—these were among the least of the good deeds which the spirit of Christ's religion taught her to perform. She was ripening daily for a better world. Her children growing around her, were hers as well by faith in Christ as by the ties of blood. Her fame went everywhere as *Electa, the mother of the faithful, the friend of the distressed.*

But now the time of trial came. Strict orders were issued from the Roman Emperor that all who professed the name of Christ should recant or suffer death. The soldiers swept through the

land in search of all who were known
as being of this faith, and thousands in
every part suffered martyrdom for their
fidelity to the cause. It was not possible that so shining a mark as Electa
should escape, and a band of soldiers
soon found their way through those
doors so long opened for the entrance of
the poor and distressed. But the captain
of the band was a Freemason, and most
loth to injure one of whose good deeds
he had heard so much. He besought
her urgently, therefore, to recant from
Christianity. He told her the recanta-
tion was a mere form, which need not
indeed affect her private opinions, and
handed her a cross which he bade her
throw upon the floor and put her foot
upon it, assuring her that he would then
leave her without danger, and make re-
port that she had recanted.

She took the cross, but it was to press
it to her bosom, to her lips, to weep
tears of love to Christ upon it, to assure

the soldier that in this sign she was more than willing to die, and that from the hour she professed the Christian religion, she had waited eagerly for this opportunity to testify her love for Christ. She told him to do his duty, whatever it was, and *Christ would give her Divine Grace to do hers.*

The family was then cast into a loathsome dungeon, where they remained for a year. Their splendid dwelling was burnt, and all their property taken away or destroyed. They were reduced to want in a single day. At the end of the year the Roman Judge came in person to their cell, and being also a Freemason, and one who had often sat lovingly under the instructions of the Grand Master, her husband, besought them yet as it was not too late, to save their lives by recanting from the faith. He pleaded with them by many arguments, by their love for their children, by the love of life and by the horrors of the death,

5

which infallibly awaited them if they persisted in their determination, to yield ere it was too late. But Electa made answer as before, and so did all her family. It was good, she said, that they for whom Christ died should give testimony to the power of his death by dying for him.

Then came the last sad scene. They were taken from the dungeon, and savagely scourged—mother, father and and children—until life barely lingered in their tortured bodies. Then they were taken in carts drawn by oxen, amidst the jeers and scorn of the people, to the nearest hill, and one by one nailed to crosses. As the meek and loving servant of Christ was left to the last, she saw her husband and children suspended until speedy death released them from their sufferings. Then came her turn, and she soon gave up her spirit to God, her last words being a prayer for pardon upon her guilty murderers.

In the next Grand Lodge St. John related her history, and as there were few present who had not shared in her kindness and hospitality, the relation was received with profound interest. At his suggestion it was agreed that the whole should be perpetuated by sign and passes as I have given them to you, and so for 1800 years, one generation to another has told the mournful yet triumphant story of the Christian martyr, Electa.

(*Here explain again, and carefully, the sign of Electa, and the manner in which the pass is given.*)

ELECTA.--2 John, i : 5.

Air.—"AULD LANG SYNE."

Her gentle hand and yielding heart,
  Shall grace our world no more;
She chose the true but better part
  Her Saviour chose before;
The Cross its gloomy load has borne,
  The grave concealed his prey,
Yet in the triumph she has won
  We cast all tears away.

This heartless world but ill can spare,
  Its jewels rich and few,
But she—most excellent and rare,
  The generous and the true—
She, in departing, left to earth,
  Such pattern of her faith,
That though her life was matchless worth,
  Even worthier was her death.

By her we learn the tenderest heart
  Is bravest to endure,—
For at the Cross HE'll not desert,
  Who all its suffering bore ;—
Among ten thousand, fairest she,
  When bleeding, dying, high
Her risen Lord proclaimed her free,
  And hailed her to the sky !

Her fame upon the wings of time,
  Through every land was swept ;
Electa's FAITH unmatched, sublime,
  Electa's NAME has kept ;
Meek, radiant one ! whose willing blood
  Her faith in Christ did seal ;
While hearts can feel and tears be stirred,
  Thy history we will tell.

They now pass to the East. W. P.
w c h. C—a c d f l i t e s d.

W. P. —The first thing to which I call
your attention is *the Signet of the Eastern Star.* This is prepared with a view
to assist the memory after a person has

taken the degree. It is well called the *Monitor of the Eastern Star*, for by its use you can recall everything that has been communicated to you. First, observe the five emblems in the centre.— The Open Bible, the Bunch of Lillies, the Sun, the Lamb, and the Lion. Each of these, as used here, is a Christian emblem, and has a proper motto attached.

The Open Bible has its motto at the bottom of the Signet, "The Word." The Bunch of Lillies is read on the right "The Lily of the Valley." The Sun is read at the lower right hand corner, "The Sun of Righteousness." The Lamb is read at the lower left hand corner, "The Lamb of God." The Lion is read on the left, "The Lion of the tribe of Judah." All these, together with the other mottoes around the sides, " The Bright and Morning Star," " The Star out of Jacob," &c., refer to the Redeemer Jesus Christ, in whom all

Christian Masons place their trust, and whose birth is alluded to in the sentences at the top, w h s h s i t e a h e t w h. These emblems will show you how much of religion there is interwoven in this beautiful Degree of the Eastern Star.

You will also see that the Star in the Signet is *five pointed.* This alludes to the Birth, Life, Death, Resurrection and Ascension of the Lord Jesus Christ.—Each point on the Star has a color of its own, the reason of which will be explained to you in due time. The names of the five characters, Jephthah's Daughter, Ruth, Esther, Martha and Electa, are seen in the different points, and the histories of these make up the Degree. Each of these has an emblem opposite, the Sword, the Sheaf, the Crown, the Broken Column, and the Joined Hands. These form a part of the histories.

S a l f h i d a a s. S m m t a o a m m w m b p, b m o o m o t f s. W a m

m s o o t s g, i i h d t r a f.—H w w h n
o a c, o s o p, a o t b o i. t p o t s. This
introduction will enable them with safety
to make use of other means of recogni-
tion, and thereby satisfy each other of
their respective Masonic claims. I will
now give you the origin of these signs.
That of J. D., or the D. S., alludes t t
m o h d. That of R, or t W. S.—
t t m o h s e b B, t s h t e o h g. That o
E. or t W. S.—a t t m o h m h a b t K i
b o h p. That o M. or t s s.—a t t m i w
s m h s o h r f B, a t d o h B. That o
E o t c S.—a t t m o h d, w w t o t c.
The color B is app to J. D., a a t t c
h o t m, a w c s s h w s w p h f h t f.
The e i t s, t b t i b w s w s.—T c Y i a
t R, t b t c o t r g i t b f o B. The e i
t s, t b f i t b f o B. The C W i a t E,
t b t c o t q r s w, w s e t p o t K. The
e a t C a S, t b e o R.—The c G i a t M.
a a t m r o h b L. The e i t b c. A a
t h u d. The C R i a t E. a i e o t b s s
u t c. The e i t j h a i t o h b h.

W a l c t h t t d, a h g o o m o ts. a m m m e h i t r i t t m. H I w i w t C. s w g t s o E. I r, a g h t p. W w t C.—I a i w, a a s, a a s r. W. P.—B b I c g y s r. I m b s t y a n i, I w t e y i t r.

W. P.—"A y a s o t e s?" C.—"I h s h s i t e." W. P.—"F w ç y h?" C.—"A h c t w h." W. P.—H y t c w? C.—I h. W. P.—W y g i t m? C.—I w w y a. W. P.—B. C.—N y b. W. P.—B y. C.—F.· W. P.—A. C.—T. W. P.—A. C.—L. F. W. P.—H t w a s? C.—i h t; f, i w b f t t c o a S, o B f t w s r t s o t d u; s, e o t l s f o o m w, w w f t c m. W. P.—H y t c m? C.—I h. W. P.—W y g i t m? C.—I w w y a. W. P.—b C.—N y b. W. P.—B y. C.—F—W. P.—a—C—t—W. P.—a—C—l.

W. P.—i t w h w b e w m t a w s i j e t h c. T i c t f b h o t E S D. A y c r p b t h i a t m t w a a t s b t t s. I w n c t c m. J. D. b s c r u h l t p h f h w.

Fataal. R.—b s f h f a w, t s m d
w t p o G w—F a t a a l. E.—b s w p
t r h c a l t s t p o G f d, o t p w t w. F
a t a,a l. M.—b s n f a m d t s p t ı t
d, w F a t a a l. A f. E.—b s j r u h h
c g n a l t s m t t h c l b a m d w f a t a a l
s l i b w e o y. A y i t v o t c a t s o G·
S s b y r. Y w n b c t s a t d, y s a t d
a a o u, a t w i t p t w t a c, b e t t a r
t, p t h t,l i a ı, t w n h b f w t c t e a a
R o a E.

I w n i y i t s a p w o t D. W y e o r f
t l, p t t c o t r, a s t. W. P. w t s o E.
T s i a g a a t w y a t a t W.P. o a m a t l.
T p w, w b g a t o o t l. W t P.—p a,
y w a a w t t t w F. Y m n s t B l a b
w t a s i o l.

INSTALLATION SERVICE.

Marshal—Most Worthy Grand President, I present you my worthy sister (or Bro.) A. B., to be installed President of this Lodge. I find her to be of good morals, true and trusty, and as she is a lover of the principles of Adoptive Masonry, I doubt not she will discharge her duties with fidelity.

W. G. P.—Worthy Sister, previous to your investiture, it is necessary that you should signify your assent to those charges and regulations which point out the duty of a President of a Lodge of Adoptive Masons.

1st. You agree to be faithful, good and true, and strictly to obey the moral law.

2d. You agree to hold in veneration

the rules and regulations of the Order of Adoptive Masonry, and of the Lodge over which you have been elected to preside, and that you will submit to the awards and resolutions of your sisters and brothers when convened, in every case consistent with the rules governing the order.

3d You agree to avoid all private piques, and quarrels, and use your influence to prevent them among your sisters and brothers.

4th. You agree to be cautious in your carriage and behavior, and courteous to your sisters and brothers, and faithful to your Lodge.

5th. You promise to respect genuine sisters and brothers, and discountenance impostors, and all dissenters from the original plan of Adoptive Masonry.

6th. You agree to promote the general good of society, to cultivate the social virtues, and to propagate the knowledge of the arts of Adoptive Masonry.

7th. You admit that no person can become a member of this Lodge without previous notice and due inquiry into their moral character.

8th. You promise that no visitors shall be admitted into this Lodge, without due examination, or producing proper vouchers of their having taken the Eastern Star Degree.

Do you submit to these charges, and promise to support these regulations?

Ans.—I do.

Sister A. B., in consequence of your cheerful conformity to the rules and regulations of this order, you are now to be installed as President of this Lodge. In full confidence of your care, skill and capacity to govern the same, I now invest you with the badge of your office.

The Bible is then presented.

From this book we have taken all the moral lessons that are taught in Adoptive Masonry. Study it carefully and it will guide you into all truth; it will direct your paths into all happiness, and point out your duty to God and to your sisters and brothers.

The chart is then presented.

This chart will guide you in your duties that are of a more hidden character see that none are permitted to look into these mysteries but such as are entitled to receive them.

Lastly you will receive in charge the by-laws of this Lodge, which you are to see carefully and punctually executed.

CHARGE TO THE WORTHY PRESIDENT.

Worthy President. The sisters and brethren having committed to your care the superintendence and government of this Lodge, you cannot be insensible of the obligations which devolve upon you as their chief officer. The honor, reputation and usefulness of your Lodge will depend on the skill and assiduity with which you manage its concerns; while the happiness of its members will be generally promoted in proportion to the zeal and ability with which you propagate the genuine principles of Adoptive Masonry. From the spirit which you have hitherto evinced, I entertain no doubt that your future conduct will be such as to merit the applause of those who have favored you by their suffrages and the testimony of a good conscience.

THE VICE PRESIDENT.

Brother Vice President.—You have been duly elected Vice President of this Lodge, and you are now invested with the badge of your office. Your regular attendance on our stated meetings is essentially necessary, as it is your duty to assist the Worthy President in the government of this Lodge, and to administer the obligation to candidates. I firmly rely on your knowledge of Adoptive Masonry, and your attachment to this Lodge, for the faithful discharge of the duties of this important trust. Look well to the same.

THE FIVE PATRONS.

Sister Patrons.—You have been elected to responsible offices, and it becomes your respective duties to represent Jephthah's Daughter, Ruth, Esther, Martha, and Electa. In these we contemplate certain exalted virtues, in their relationship to our Lord Jesus Christ, that perfect exemplar of all virtue. The benefits of Adoptive Masonry are mainly for the female sex. They are its glory and crown, and its value consists in the spirit with which they enter it, and the grace they throw around it, and as you, my sisters, are to be the representatives of this ‖☰‖, it should be your constant duty to so regulate your lives, that the honor, glory and reputation of the Eastern Star may be firmly established and the world at large convinced of its good effects.

Sister First Patron.—Are you willing to covenant your honor as a woman, that you will faithfully discharge the duties of the office of first Patron.

It is well. Receive the badge of your office. Its color, blue, which is sym·bolical of the hue of the distant mountains under Judah's clear sky, and it serves to remind us of the two months stay made by Adah in the mountains while fortifying her mind against the terrors of a violent death. May you wear it with pleasure to yourself and honor to our Society.

Sister Second Patron.—Are you willing to covenant your honor as a woman that you will faithfully discharge the duties of the office of Second Patron.

It is well. Receive the badge of your office. Its color, yellow, which is the hue of the barley fields on the plains of Judah, and reminds us that in that place of harvest all the prayers of Ruth were

6

answered, her faith rewarded and her
trust in God vindicated, May you wear
it with pleasure to yourself and honor to
our Society.

Sister Third Patron.—Are you willing to covenant your honor as a woman
that you will faithfully discharge the duties of the office of Third Patron.

It is well. Receive the badge of your
office. Its color, white, which is the hue
of the silken robes of Esther, it serves
to remind us that, in the spotless purity
of Christ, we can alone expect to find
favor at the Throne of God. May you
wear it with pleasure to yourself and
honor to our Society.

Sister Fourth Patron.—Are you willing to covenant your honor as a woman
that you will faithfully discharge the duties of the office of Fourth Patron.

It is well. Receive the badge of your
office. Its color, green, which is the
hue of spring, also the hue that covers
every grave, as with a mantle. It serves

to remind us that as Lazarus came forth at the command of Christ, so shall we, at the spring-time of the Resurrection, be summoned from our graves by the same commanding voice. May you wear it with pleasure to yourself and honor to our Society.

Sister Fifth Patron.—Are you willing to covenant your honor as a woman that you will faithfully discharge the duties of the office of Fifth Patron?

It is well. Receive the badge of your office. Its color, red, which is the hue of blood and wine. It should serve to remind us to dispense of our temporal means to the poor, even as the Redeemer gave his heart's blood to save us from eternal death. May you wear it with pleasure to yourself and honor to our Society.

Sisters.—Do you submit to all these requirements, and promise to observe and practice them faithfully? It is well. I accept it.

THE SECRETARY.

Sister A. B.—You have been elected Secretary of this Lodge, and are now invested with the badge of your office. It is your duty to keep a record of all its proceedings, to receive all monies paid into the Lodge and pay them over to the Treasurer, taking her receipt for the same. Your good inclination to Adoptive Masonry and this Lodge, will, I hope, induce you to discharge the duties of your office with fidelity, and by so doing you will merit the esteem and applause of your sisters and brothers.

THE TREASURER.

Sister A. B.—You have been elected Treasurer of this Lodge, and are now invested with the badge of your office. It is your duty to receive all monies from the hands of the Secretary, keep a just

and regular account of the same, and
pay them out by order of the Worthy
President, with the consent of the Lodge
I trust your regard for this mystic family, will prompt you to the faithful discharge of the duties of your office.

THE CONDUCTOR.

Sister A. B.—You are chosen Conductor of this Lodge, and are now invested with the badge of your office.
It is your duty to guide the footsteps of
the candidates in their unknown mean-
derings, and assist the Worthy President in the explanations of the symbolic
mysteries of Adoptive Masonry; also to
introduce all who shall be admitted as
visitors. Look well to the discharge of
these important duties.

THE GUARD.

Sister A. B.—You are chosen Guard
over this Lodge, and are now invested
with the badge of your office. It is your

duty to obey the behest of your superiors in office, and faithfully deliver any messages that may be intrusted to your care, also to see that the avenues of approach are duly guarded while the Lodge is called from refreshment to labor. Let vigilance be your constant watchword.

THE SENTINEL.

Brother A. B. —You are chosen sentinel of this Lodge, and I now invest you with the jewel of your office. As the key is placed in the hands of the Sentinel to enable him the more effectually to guard the avenues of approach to our mystic family fireside, so it should ever morally serve as a constant admonition to us, to set a guard at the entrance of our thoughts, to place a watch at the door of our lips, and to post a sentinel over our actions, thereby excluding every unqualified and unworthy thought, word or deed, and preserving a conscience void of offence toward God and toward man. Your early and punctual attendance will afford the best proof of your zeal and attachment for the institution.

ADDRESS TO THE LODGE.

Sisters and Brethren of———Eastern Star Lodge:—Such is the nature of our constitutions, that some must of necessity rule and teach, so others must of course learn to submit and obey. Humility in both is an essential duty. The officers who are appointed to govern your Lodge, are sufficiently conversant with the rules of propriety to avoid exceeding the powers with which they are intrusted, and you are of too generous a disposition to envy their preferment. I therefore trust that you will have but one aim—to please each other—and unite in the grand design of being happy and communicating happiness.

Finally, may you long enjoy every satisfaction and delight which disinterested friendship can afford, may the principles of Adoptive Masonry be transmitted through your Lodge, pure and unimpaired from generation to generation.